Serendipity & Me

Serendipity & Me

BY

JUDITH L. ROTH

SCHOLASTIC INC.

ISBN 978-0-545-62621-7

12 11 10 9 8 7 6 5 4 3 2 1   13 14 15 16 17 18/0

Printed in the U.S.A.   40

First Scholastic printing, September 2013

Set in Excelsior

Book design by Nancy Brennan

The three poems quoted in *Serendipity and Me*, "The Look," "I Shall Not Care," and a selection from "A November Night," come from the collection *Love Songs*, by Sara Teasdale (New York: The Macmillan Company, 1917).

FOR MARC, in gratitude and love—from that first dorm kitty to children, grown, our life together has been a blessing. . . .

✣

ser•en•dip•i•ty (ser-ən-'*di*-pə-tē) n. 1. The ability to make lucky discoveries. 2. A happy surprise.

kit•ty ('*ki*-tē) n. What you call a cat when you like it.

✣

I remember
      my mom quoting
      "The fog comes
      on little cat feet"
And my dad replying
      "More like big elephant feet"

      because the fog here
      in Central California
      is a dense gray wall
      that bellows in its silence

Tule
      sounds like toolie
      named for grass
      growing in wetlands
      where this fog forms

Tule
      sounds like boonies
      like out in the boonies

where this fog is thickest

like out in the Tule boonies
where my mom
was lost to me

forever

It starts as a tickle

    in the back of my throat.

But I can't pay attention

    because Mrs. Detweiler

    (the other sixth-grade teacher, not mine)

    is going over prerehearsal notes,

    is saying, *Channel your mother, Sara,*

    thinking she's being cute

    because you only channel someone

    who's dead.

She doesn't know, I guess.

My teacher shoots her a look

    and tells me, *Just be gentle*

    when you tuck in the Lost Boys. . . .

    Wendy is very nurturing.

I look down at Miss Conglin from the stage

    and put my hand on my neck

· that feels wider than usual.
Put my hand on my neck
where my throat feels
like it's swallowing knives

and wish someone
was mothering me.

Today is Monday of our
          last week of rehearsing
          before the performance
          Saturday night.
Our first day for dress rehearsal. . . .

I am in a nightgown
          in front of Garrett.
It is long and thick and white
          and buttoned high on my neck.
          But still . . .
          it is a little embarrassing.

He sees me blush and says,
          Are you kidding me?
          So you're in a nightgown—
          I have to wear freaking tights!

And just like that
          he gets me smiling again.
He sees the smile and jumps into

his Peter Pan pose,
fists on hips
and chest held high.
How clever I am! he quotes from his lines.

And I am about to give him
a gentle Wendy-bashing
but I am too tired

and it's not the nightgown
that's making me feel sleepy.

My best friend Taylor is offstage
      in her huge sheepdog costume
      and I see Kelli lean over
      and say something to her.

I can tell Taylor is annoyed
      when she makes
      an elbow-space between them.

After the scene, I ask her
      What did Kelli say to you?

She lifts the shaggy dog head
      so she can talk without shouting
      and shakes out her dark hair.
      She said you were dying out here
      that she should have been Wendy
      that you were typecast
         because you're blonde.

I sigh.   All I can come up with is

Wendy's not always a blonde.

Taylor says, *She's an idiot either way.*
    You're the best one on this stage.

I wish.

    Right now I almost feel
    like I'm dying out here
    for real.

By the time rehearsal is over
      my head is pounding
      and my eyes feel dry-as-the-desert
      even though my nose
      has sprung a leak.

Miss Conglin starts to snap at me
      because I'm taking so long
      getting my stuff together

      then she takes a harder look
      and lays her cool hand
      against my forehead.
      Her mouth twists.
      Someone coming to pick you up?

I nod.

She fingers the studs high on her ear.
Get some rest, Sara.

And drink a lot.

Does your dad keep juice in the house?

I shrug.

Miss Conglin pats me on the back.

See you tomorrow.

But she doesn't sound

like she believes it.

Tuesday morning. . . .
In four days I'm supposed to be
        asking Peter Pan
        Boy, why are you crying?

        but my throat is so raw
        I can barely whisper.

Dad has fixed up the couch in the family room
        with extra pillows
        and the daisy quilt Mom made me
        when I was four.

I have the remote control
        a glass of juice
        a box of tissues
        and a phone to call Mrs. Whittier
        from next door if I need something.

I am wishing I could just sleep and not feel
        the head pounding

heat flashing
throat stabbing.

But I hurt too much to sleep.

And my mind is replaying
the way Garrett squirms and laughs
when I sew the shadow
back on Peter Pan's foot.

Who will do that now?

What if his tickled smile
is for someone other
than me?

I keep seeing that smile.

Maybe if Mom was here
        I wouldn't ask her.
But since she's not
        I wish I could ask
        Why do I feel this way?

I can't talk to Taylor
        because she still
        punches boys in the arms
        like that's what they're made for.

And I can't talk to Dad
        because he's Dad.

Already bad enough Mom can't
        see me in my first ever play. . . .

If Mom were here she would
        tuck my stuffed kitty next to me

watch a movie with me
keep my juice refilled
check my temperature
     with her lips
     on my forehead . . .

explain to me about boys.

Wednesday—two days into this illness.
I am still not feeling better.

Dad had to go to college chapel—
he was presenting something about
poetry and spirituality—
so Mrs. Whittier stayed back.

She has just come to check on me
when Dad gets home.
She leans over to take
the thermometer from my mouth
her long silver hair swinging forward.

She reads the numbers
and hands Dad the thermometer.
You might want to call the doctor
she says quietly.

She is trying her best not to interfere

so she can stay in our lives.

I know this because it's
exactly what she told me
when I asked where she'd been
lately.

Dad looks at the thermometer,
        mutters, *Still 102,*
        and reaches for the phone.
He pushes my bangs off my forehead
        while he waits for an answer.

        He looks surprised
        by how wet it is.
My freshmen were supposed to come over
        tomorrow night, he says.
        Looks like I'll have to reschedule.

I look out the window
        and across the street
        at the small college campus.

Some crazy kids are braving the March chill
        and having an early water fight

between classes.

I watch a biker duck under
a stream from a water blaster
and land in the bushes
under a girls' dorm window.

I should be sad we'll be missing
    the freshman meeting

    the only time our house
    has life in it.

But right now I
    just don't care.

The quick strep test—

       the one where you
       sit outside the doctor's lab
       and feel like a germ factory
       and gag on the swab
       the nurse sticks down your throat—

       comes back negative

       which means it's a virus
       and there's nothing they can do for me
       and I have to just get through it.

Miss Conglin calls
       to ask how I'm doing.

Dad tells her I won't be in school
       for at least another day
       that I'm really not doing well

       and I'm motioning for him to

stop talking
stop making her think
I won't be ready for the play

and he doesn't get it
thinks I want to talk to her

hands me the phone.

Sara?

> I can hear music in the background
> something with a heavy beat.

Sara? How are you?

I want to say, Horrible.

> I want to say, Ready to perform.
> I want to say, Please don't replace me.
> I can still be Wendy.
> I can still fly
>> second to the right
>> and straight on till morning.

What I say is *Fine*.

> It comes out a whisper.
> It comes out a scratch.

Oh, sweetie, Miss Conglin says.

> *Get better.*

I'll send Taylor over
with your makeup work.

But we both know
    schoolwork
    is not the real issue
    here.

If I get well in time
    I will be the perfect Wendy.

    I will be so nurturing
    the Lost Boys will miss their mothers.

    John and Michael
    will forget I'm only their sister.

    I will even help Peter Pan
    grow up gracefully.

This is what I think
    when my daisy quilt becomes
    too hot to lie under
    and then not warm enough
    when I'm shaking from chills.

If I get well in time

I will be the best mother.

Even though
I don't have anyone
anymore
to show me
how.

Taylor comes over after school Thursday
     her arms full of books.
     She dumps them on the floor
     beside the couch
        and backs away.
     All the work,
        Tuesday through Thursday.
     If we get more tomorrow,
        I'll bring it.

I look up at her through puffy eyes.
     What's happening at rehearsal?

Taylor softens her
     force-field-against-germs attitude.
     Miss Conglin put in Kelli for now.

Is she any good?

Taylor shrugs.

She knows the part.

I decide to ask Taylor something
      I'm not sure she'd even notice.
      Is, um . . . does Garrett
      still act goofy?

Taylor rolls her eyes.
      He's always a goof.
      Kelli laughs her head off at him.

Just what I was afraid of.

It is time for drastic measures.
I need to get well now
    so I can make it
    to the last practice tomorrow.

It used to be our nightly ritual.
    Mom and Dad would come to my room
    at bedtime
    and we'd pray together.

After Mom died
    things were so confused for a while
    and then one night
    I asked Dad to come pray again.

He stood in the doorway for a minute
    then sat on the edge of my bed.
    You start, he said.

But when I prayed
    Bless Mommy and Daddy

a sob burst out of him
then he laid his hand on my head
and lurched out of the room.

I didn't ask again.

So I ask alone tonight
Please, God.

I wake up on the couch
     to sounds in the kitchen.
     Dad?

Just me, Mrs. Whittier calls.
Then she steamrollers in
     with a steaming bowl.
     Hungry?
     Here's some chicken bone soup.

My mind is cloudy with sleep and sickness.
     What day is it?

Friday.   *I've got ceramics lab at noon*
     so one of the college girls
     will be coming later
     to check on you.

I force my zombie brain to think.

The play's tomorrow.

Yes.

Her drab pottery work shirt
suits the mood because
by the sympathy dripping off her face
I can tell I won't be in the play.
It is too late

and Neverland

has a whole different meaning
for me now.

I'm pretty sure Jocelyn
        was one of Dad's freshmen
        when Mom died.

Now she's a serious senior.
        Majoring in psychology, she tells me
        dark eyes wide with compassion.

She wants to know how I feel
        about everything.
Either I'm too sick to guard my mouth
        or she's going to be
        really good at this.

        Because I tell her everything
        I've been keeping quiet inside me.

I tell her how much I love *Peter Pan* the play
        and how much I like Peter Pan the boy.
I tell her how much I miss my mother

and how my dad's a mess of sadness.

I tell her how lonely I am
      in my own house.

I lumber off the couch
      to show her my room.

She asks about the cats.

There are pictures of cats
on every wall
of my pale-pink room.

Besides my cuddly stuffed kitty,
lions and tigers and cougars
lie helter-skelter on my covers.

Cat-head slippers peek out
from under the bed.

Where's your real cat?
Jocelyn asks.

I don't have one.

She raises her eyebrows in a question.

Mom always said, Ask your father

and Dad always said, No.

She purses her lips and then her look rests
       on my book of Mom Tales.
       What's this?

Mom used to make up fairy tales
       and write them down for me.
       I show her the first page.
       This one's about Mom and Dad.

Beginnings

Once upon a time there was a magical professor who spun poems around his students. The poems gave his students wings. Sometimes they found themselves hovering in the air as if in a dream. One of his students was a girl named for dreams.

Aislinn was born with a hunger for words. She took to the winged poems like she was created to fly. She drank the words in. She swallowed them whole. And she soared.

Each time Aislinn heard the professor speak, her wings grew stronger and she flew toward paradise. But the spell never lasted. When she left the professor, her wings drooped and she drifted to the ground.

She knew she must keep the professor and his magical words with her forever. So Aislinn decided to cast a spell on him.

Her plan was a web of beauty. She reversed the spell he placed on his class and spun her own poems around him. Aislinn's poems captured his heart and sent his soul soaring with dreams of her. And when he was completely under her spell, Aislinn showed him her own dreams of flying with him forever. She offered him the wings of her soul with a book of Love Songs.

The magical professor took the book. He took the book and read her heart and fell into her soul.

The sweetest spell of all.

Jocelyn looks puzzled.
     Wow—your mom was a student?

Yeah.   *They were supposed to live*
        happily ever after.
        But there wasn't any ever after.

Jocelyn's grown-up mask slips a bit
        and she looks like she wishes
        she didn't know so much
        about me

        or that she knew
        what to say
        now.

If this were a TV show counseling session
        now would be the perfect chance
        to say, Our time is up.

But she doesn't have the

counselor's skill yet
of ending a conversation.

Jocelyn pets my stuffed kitty
        pulls at the neck of her sweater
        and smiles at me
        shyly.

Beneath the fairy tale book
    is a white baby blanket
    decorated with pastel balloons.
I wrap a satin frayed edge
    around my wrist
    and climb into bed,
    too tired to move back to the couch.

Jocelyn eyes the blanket
    and I can tell she's curious

    but this is something
    I will keep to myself.

My eyes close
    the comfort of the silky edging
    touching my skin.

The blanket has been used as
    a belt, a kerchief

a veil, an apron
while Mom and I acted out fairy tales.

Used as a token, a flag
a banner, a snowfall
while Mom read poetry to me
and I dreamed of performing the words.

The blanket was here with me
        through it all.

It's still here.
        But Mom is not.

I must be delirious
       because when I wake up Saturday
       I think I can do it.
       Be in the play tonight.

I go to the bathroom and open
       the drawer that was my mom's.

       It's still full of her stuff.
       Not like her side of the closet
       that only has clanging hangers
       since Mrs. Whittier
       called my grandparents
       to come and help Dad let go
       last year.

I rattle through her makeup
       and find what I think I need
       for the stage.
       I shower and do my hair

then play with eyeliner, mascara

powder, blush.

Dad knocks on the door.

Everything all right in there?

I unlatch the door

and let it swing slowly open.

Dad glances in

then freezes.

He looks like he's seen a ghost.

His face scares me
                  so I look in the mirror
                  to see what he sees.

And I almost see her.
                  Eyes defined, cheekbones sculpted.
                  If I squint, the messy makeup
                  smooths out
                  makes me look older.

                  So much more like my mom
                  than ever before.

I turn back to Dad
                  and his eyes change like he
                  recognizes me again.
He shakes his head.
                  Sorry about the play.
                  You know you can't go, right?
                  He makes the dorky sad puppy face

that used to make me smile.

I tell him Yes
and close the door.

Then I watch myself in the mirror
as the tears start falling

and I learn too soon
what happens to makeup
when you cry.

Grandma and Grandpa call
>>three hours before the play starts.
>>In my mind
>>>>I can see them
>>>>leaning toward the speakerphone.
>>Grandpa listening with his good ear.
>>Grandma doing most of the talking.
>>*Hi, Honey—just wanted to wish you luck*
>>>>*before your big performance.*
>>*Wish we could be there!*
They live in the hills of Pennsylvania
>>on the other side of the country.
>>Too far away to sense
>>my impending heartbreak.

Thanks—but I'm too sick to do it.
>>I try to keep the catch out of my voice.

Oh, Honey, Grandma says. *Oh, I'm so sorry.*

What are you sick with?

A stupid virus.
>I tell them all my symptoms
>and they both make sympathetic noises.
>Grandma tells me how sorry they are
>and they hope I get better soon
>and she asks to talk to Dad.

I can tell by Dad's responses
>he feels awkward with them.
His own parents do service work overseas
>so Mom's parents are the ones
>Mrs. Whittier called last year.

I listened from my room
>when they had their face-to-face chat.
The words I heard from Dad were
>*Intrusive.*
>*Handling it.*
>*I need more time.*

The words I heard from them were

Counseling.
Grieving too long.
Not good for Sara.

Now Dad says, *Yes, yes.*
    I'm taking good care of her.
    I will.

He hangs up and turns to me.
    They send you their love.

Somehow   even that small phrase
    sends a tear
    down my cheek.

I try and keep a low profile
　　　　the rest of the day.
Dad is not comfortable with tears
　　　　and I don't feel like
　　　　dealing with him
　　　　not dealing with me.

Now　　　　out there in the world
　　　　the play is going on
　　　　without me.

　　　　A Kelli-Wendy
　　　　is following my Peter Pan
　　　　through the night air.

　　　　Not me.

I lie on the couch
　　　　like an old sub sandwich

forgotten and soggy.

My daisy quilt is damp with tears
and used tissues.

Even the cards
Dad's artsy students made me
are wet from weeping,
the homemade paper wilting,
the inked letters running.

I'm a mess not just because
I'm painfully sick
and missing the play. . . .

There on the TV screen
a sun-bright woman
gently lays her arm
across the shoulders
of her daughter.

My heart wails
and I wonder if she can hear me
from heaven . . .

wonder if she knows
what I'm going through.

It's no use.
I can't stop crying.

Dad comes in with some apple juice
sees my tears
and stops

totally clueless

about what to do.

I feel a sob coming up from my chest
but it startle-stops
when our doorbell rings.

No one is there when Dad answers—
only a little white kitten
who darts into our house
like a paper airplane.

Dad chases it around madly
and they look so funny
I quit crying
and start laughing.

Dad stares at me for a moment
surprised and relieved
and when he finally catches the kitten
he puts it into my arms and says,
Serendipity, Sara.

Someone's brought you a blessing
for a visit.

The little fluffball licks my nose
and suddenly
nothing else matters.

All I care about now
is making this visit
last forever.

Dad has never told me
why I can't have a cat.

He has just told me No
and turned his face away
stared out the window
or into his book
his mouth held
like there are marbles
resting on his tongue

like the marbles
are years of tears

petrified.

Dad goes out the front door.
I hear his footsteps
scrape past the empty carport
then stop.

I picture him
scanning the horizon
searching for the troublemaker
who dropped a cat
into our lives.

By the time he comes back
the kitten is already
kneading a soft spot
in my stomach.

Any ideas who left the cat?
he asks.

I shake my head.

His eyes squint
into his thinking expression

figuring a way
I suppose

to send the cat back.

It is lucky for me
        I'm sick and sad.

Now may be my only chance.
        Can't I keep it?
        Please?

The shades come down over Dad's eyes.
        You know cats aren't an option.

For tonight, at least?
You can't throw it out in the cold.
I wipe at my mascara-running eyes
        and tearstained cheeks
        to remind him
        who he's dealing with
        tonight.

Dad sighs
        looks at his watch.
        I guess it is pretty late.

I can take it to the shelter tomorrow.

I kiss the kitten's forehead
     and it straight-arms its paw
     on my mouth.
Boy or girl? I ask.

Dad sighs again, then checks.
     I think it's a girl.

Maybe looking at the end
     reminds him.
I hope she's litter-trained.
I'd better go find a box
     and some newspaper.

My heart says
     And a way.
          I'd better
          find a way
          that she can stay.

At least she is mine
        for tonight.

I can pretend she'll be mine
        forever.

I'll begin with her name. . . .

She's white as a snowball
        but she's warm
        not frozen.

She's squishy and soft and sweet
        as a marshmallow.

But she's delicate as an orchid
        graceful as a ballerina
        miraculous as an angel.

I can't believe my luck

that she's here with me.

I guess Dad named her
          after all.

Serendipity.

It's been three years.
You'd think we'd be better
     by now. . . .

Dad does the best he can

          but I remember
          cheek-kisses
          soft as velvet.

          I remember
          a gentle voice saying
          It's all right, honey bunny,
          I'm here.

          I remember
          sweet smells and a cushy robe
          when we hugged after her bath.

Tonight in my room

I sprinkle Mom's scented powder
on Serendipity
and I lay my cheek on her side

and I remember

soft.

Serendipity is curled on my pillow.
        Her kneading claws
                catch on the eyelet edging
        her throat rattles from purrs
        her head is snuggled into my neck
        so sweet it makes
                my heart hurt.

I think—
        This is what I've been missing
        all these years.

I think—
        I don't want to miss this
        anymore.

I think—
        No is not a fair word
        when you're a kid
        without a mother
        and you need something soft
        to hold on to.

I reach for the phone
     dial Taylor's number.
     Dad would say ten is too late
     but I know Taylor won't care.

She answers so cheerfully
     I have to bury the phone in my quilt.

     She must have had a blast
     being Nana in the play.

     I feel a twinge
     but it doesn't matter as much anymore.
        Shhh, I say.
        This is secret.

What? she asks, suddenly quiet.

How was the play?

Great—what's the secret?

Patience is not one of her virtues.

I have a cat for the night, I say.
    And I need to keep her forever.

Taylor is always ready.
    What do you need me to do?

This is what we work out—
    Taylor will pretend
    her mom is considering
    adopting the kitten.
    She just needs a week
    to think
    to work out the details.

But this will not happen.

Dad doesn't know Taylor's mother
    is allergic to cats.

Dad doesn't know
    if we keep Serendipity
    for a week
    he will get over his No
    because he will fall in love
    with this kitten.

He will get over his No

because he will see
how much
I need her.

He will get over his No.

He has to.

Serendipity has scrambled eggs
      for breakfast
      this first morning.

She is a miracle cure.
I feel well enough for eggs myself.

      Well enough to eat
      at the kitchen table with Dad
      while we watch Serendipity
      nibble near the fridge.

She pats her eggs like they're
      dead mice,
      like she wishes
      they'd get up and run.

Then she chomps them down
      and licks her bowl.

Just like you used to. . . .

Remember?
Dad says
his voice holding memories
        of high chairs and laughter.

His hand opens soft
        like he's letting
                something
                        go.

As soon as she's finished eating
          Serendipity comes close
          and looks skyward at me.
She gazes with such innocence—
          a baby with one blue
                    and one green eye.
My brain tells me to leave her there
          out of Dad's view.
My heart tells me to pick her up.
          I follow my heart.

Dad stares at the fluffy kitten
          washing herself on my lap
          and his eyes close.
          He crumples his napkin
          before he's finished eating
          and stands.

          I can tell he's ready
          to be tough.

I can tell he's ready
to break my heart

by taking her away.

I start talking
    as quick
     as I can.

I called Taylor last night, I begin
> and I tell him how she might
> be able to take Serendipity in a week.
> *That's okay, isn't it?* I ask
>> *We can keep her that long, right?*

Dad's face closes up.
> *Sara, we talked about this.*
> *The cat goes today.*

But she could have a home.
> My voice is squeaking.
> I grab at a statistic I read once.
> *Seventy percent of cats*
> *in shelters* die, *Dad.*

Dad clears his throat.
> *And what happens if Taylor*
> *can't take her?*
> *It'll be even harder for you*

to let her go after a week.

I—I'll put up posters, too.
    The first person who wants her
    can have her.
I'll find someone—she's so sweet
    someone will want her.
Dad, I croak out the plea,
    she needs a family.

Dad looks like I gutted him
    with the word *family*.
    Or maybe with the word *die*.
Now I know what writers mean
    when they say *hollow eyes*.

His eyes are like the deep craggy holes
    in broken trees

    and they're pointed
    right at me.

I feel my lip start to tremble   again.

    I think he's going to say No.
    I think he's going to break my heart
        with his own crushed one

    but he puts his hand on his mouth.

He stands up   I think

so he won't have to look at me.

Then he kisses the top of my head
    like a surrender.

    You're not playing fair, Sara.
    He tries for a laugh.
    I'll bet you got the flu on purpose.

He doesn't wait to see if I smile.

Dad can't say Yes to a cat
      but he also didn't say No.
      That's as good as a Yes for now.

My heart starts to lift
      until I remember
      the dark in his eyes.

And when Dad leaves the room
      it feels like
      something left the very air
         of the kitchen.

      The smell of eggs
      still lingers
      but it's an empty smell.

On the sun-spattered floor
      where Serendipity has jumped down
      to chase shadows

there is depth
and texture
and warmth.

But here in this breathing space
    where Dad left

    there is nothing.

I peek around the corner
>   and find him at his sad place
>   staring at the bookshelves
>   poets ordered by alphabet.
Are we going to church this morning?
>   I ask softly
>   just to say something.

He doesn't turn around.
>   *One more day to recover.*
>   *You can go to school tomorrow.*

Then he reaches out his finger
>   and taps the binding of a slender book
>   hooks the book and levers it down
>   like a drawbridge
>   returning
>   to its resting place.

I feel fine now, I say
>   wanting to move him

in a different direction
like he's moved the book.

He takes the book
without looking at me
goes alone into his room

and shuts the door.

At first the morning feels as thick
      as the terrible Tule fog.

I can't stand it when Dad is like this.

He can suck the joy out of a room
      in seconds
      just by looking mournful.

Sometimes I want to say
      She's dead, Dad.
      Get over it.

But then I remember
      I want something soft, too.

Serendipity changes the air.
She trips and leaps and dodges and twirls
      and then falls in my lap to sleep

      her face so sweet and fluffy

her breath a gentle stir.

She is good for me.
    I know that.

She'd be good for him, too.

Already this morning
        she's made herself at home.
She likes to see where she fits in.

I follow her as she
        squeezes into small boxes
        dallies in open drawers
        slithers into sacks
        cozies herself in closets.

We play hide-and-seek and I find her
        in my boot   in my basket
    in my backpack   in my bowl.

I can pour her like pudding
        into any shape of container.

She spreads out soft like Jell-O.

She fills up any mold.

I call Taylor.

     You have to see her.
     She's so amazing.

Taylor says   *I'm supposed to be*
     keeping Mandy busy
     while Mom fixes
        the chicken coop. . . .
Her voice drops in volume.
     We'll bike over real quick, okay?

It seems like Taylor's
     my only easy friend.
     Other girls still look away from me
     whenever a mother is mentioned.

Taylor moved here
     after my mom died.
     Taylor never knew her
     like these other girls did

these other girls who look at me
and what they see is
what could happen
to them.

Like motherlessness
is a disease.

Taylor rides up on an old blue bike
  her little sister trailing behind.
  We can't stay long.
  Mom has plans.

She swings off her bike
  and hauls Mandy wild-haired off hers.
  Where is the cutie-pie?

I turn to show Serendipity's tiny face
  peeking out of my sweatshirt pocket.

Taylor and Mandy both say *Aw*
  and hold their hands out.
I give Serendipity to Taylor
  and she holds her close to Mandy
  so they can both enjoy
  the miracle of kittyness.

She sniffs their hands delicately

a bloodhound looking for clues
about these hands
that hold chickens,
bunnies and ducks.
Taylor's menagerie.

Taylor holds Serendipity like a baby,
    wears the kitten on her head like a hat
    then hands her to me.
I believe this is yours.

Dad pokes his head out the door
      as Taylor and Mandy
      get back on their bikes.
Taking a test-drive with the kitten?
      he asks them.

Mandy looks confused
      and wobbles on her training wheels.
      Taylor rides between
      Mandy's confusion and Dad's view.
      Yeah, she's a cutie, Mr. James.
      Gotta go, though.
      See you!

Taylor gives Mandy's bike a shove
      to get her started
      and they ride off
      then Taylor circles back
      and hands me a paper
            from her pocket.
      Forgot to bring you
            the assignments Friday.

We would fail as spies.
Someone paying attention
    would notice the fishy vibe in the air,
    Taylor's nonanswer
       to the implied question.
But this one time
    Dad's distraction with sadness
    works in my favor.

He doesn't notice a thing.

Dad's already closed up in his room
        by the time I go into the house.

I put Serendipity
        on the back of the couch
        and lie down.
        I look at the note.

Sara,
- *Start looking for an interesting picture of*
  your family to use as a writing prompt—due
  Wednesday.
- *Middle Ages unit: Read pgs. 131–133*
  in Social Studies book
- *We'll get you caught up on the rest after you get*
  back to school. Feel better!
        Miss Conglin

It really is assignments

not the hoped-for sly note from Taylor
with more ideas on kitten-keeping.

I'm starting to get hungry.
        I go into the kitchen
        looking to see if Serendipity follows.
        She scampers after me
        like a puppy.

        I open some cupboards
        rattle some pans

        hoping Dad will come out
                and feed us some lunch.

I hear his door swing open
and his face appears near the fridge.

He's back—all of him
not just his sadness.
How does mac and cheese sound?

And because I spent so much time
in front of the TV this week
I say, *Super-duper.*

I open the boxes for him
and fish out the cheese envelopes
while he cuts
apple slices for our fruit
and circles of hot dogs
for the macaroni.

A hot dog circle rolls onto the ground
and Serendipity pounces.
I reach down to grab

then decide to let her eat it.
On my way up,
something catches my eye
in Dad's room.
The book he took
is lying in his sheets.
I remember seeing the title
when he pulled it down—
Love Songs.

Now I realize
I've heard that title before . . .
in Mom's fairy tale.

Sometime soon
I must get up the nerve
to ask my dad
a few questions.

The doorbell rings
    while we're still eating.

I hop up to answer
    wiping grease off my fingers
    from sneaking extra bites of hot dog
      to Serendipity.

It's Garrett
    the one I was supposed to be
    flying to Neverland with
    last night.

He looks at me with Peter Pan eyes
    as he hands me a DVD case.
    Miss Conglin asked me
    to bring this to you, he says.
      My dad recorded the play last night.
He looks down like he's reading a note
    on the skateboard at his side.
    Glances up sideways.

Sorry you couldn't be there.

I try to think of something clever to say
      but I'm so nervous
      the best I can come up with is
      How did it go?

Garrett straightens
      strikes a flying pose.
      His stardust hair
      swishes across his forehead.
      We were awesome.
Too late, he tries to look modest.
      See you tomorrow?

Tomorrow, I say
      offhand.

      But I feel
      the same lurch I felt
      that first time in rehearsal

      when he pulled the arrow
      out of my heart.

The rain starts after lunch
     drizzling slowly
     down the kitchen windows
     making it warmer inside
     somehow.

     Fortunately
     making the hanging of
     free kitten posters
     impractical
     for now.

We pile on the couch
     to watch the play.

We're like an ice-cream sundae—
     Dad lying on one side
     me on the other.
     Dad ignoring the
     marshmallow
     topping.

Kelli plays a different Wendy
    than I did.
    Older or louder or something.

When Wendy offers Peter a kiss
    and Peter holds out his hand . . .

    Kelli should have paused longer
    before handing him the thimble.

    It would take time to think
    how not to shame him—
    for not knowing what a kiss was.

I watch closely for a while
    hoping to see her make other mistakes
    even though I know that's mean.

I think she got the mothering part down
    but I was more graceful in the flying

and I feel like I was more
Peter Pan's Wendy.

I watch to see if Garrett gives Kelli
the same sweet mischievous glances
he gave me.

The camera is too far away
to tell.

I watch as much as I can stand.
But when Peter hands the thimble kiss
        back to Wendy
        and they turn away
        with tortured looks

        that is enough.

I wanted to share tortured looks
        with Peter.
I wanted to fly out my window
        and get shot down by the Lost Boys.
I wanted to fight with Tinker Bell
        and get captured by Hook
        and walk the pirates' plank.

I wanted Peter
        to fly in my window

        one
                last
                        time.

I hit Stop on the DVD
      and throw the remote.

Dad just looks at me
      then he pats my leg and says,
      Well, enough of that, I guess.
He goes into his study
      muttering something about test grades.

I sigh and slide onto the floor
      to collect the batteries
      that fell out of the remote.

      I had a favorite line in the play
      when I sprawled leaning like this
      on the stage.

      I say it softly, now.
      Don't go, Peter,
      I know such lots of stories.

But Peter Pan is gone

and there's no
getting that chapter back.

I throw myself on the couch.

Serendipity bounces up in the air
        from the impact and then
        gets a crazy look on her face.

She races out of the room
        slides around in the kitchen.
        She can't get traction.

        She needs sneakers
        on her slippery feet.

        In an instant she's back.

She takes a mighty leap
        and lands like a Velcro jumper
        limbs splayed

against the side of the couch.

She's stuck.

I can't help laughing,
     she looks so ridiculous.

I wish I had my camera handy.
     I would catch this moment forever
     put it on the mantle

     make it part of our family memory.

Dad leans out of his study door.
>*Better start making those posters,*
>*don't you think?*

It's like he can't stand to hear laughter
    in this house

    like he has to squash
    any happiness.

And now I have to advertise
    a free kitten
    to whoever is able
    to keep her.

    Anyone not like me.

This was a stupid idea.

I wonder how I can make Serendipity

seem undesirable.

Impossible.

But there might be
    something I could do. . . .

It comes as a brilliant flash—
        I will make the posters
        with the right phone number
        and show them to Dad.

But when I put up the posters
        I'll change the number one
        to a four

        so anyone
        who dares to call
        will get the wrong number.

        This should foil
        anyone who tries to take
        my slipper-sized kitten
        away.

I surprise myself

with my own deception.
I never used to be sneaky.

But now there's a cat at stake.

A cat who's still stuck
        to the side of the couch.

I take a pretend picture
        and mime placing a tiny print
        across the room on the mantel

        nestled among the rest
                of the family pictures.

I suddenly remember
        the pictures of family life
        I need for school.
I glance back at the mantel
        to see if those will do.

There is a picture of toddler me in a pumpkin patch

        seven-year-old me in a redwood grove

        kindergarten me on Santa's lap

        baby me propped against a teddy bear
        on our same old blue couch.

I unlatch Serendipity from the couch
        and take her with me to look closer.

No pictures of Mom
        no pictures of Dad

only pictures of me
from before Mom died.

In the back of my mind is a memory—
a silver frame set here
that Mom used to change every year
with a new family picture.

I wonder when that picture disappeared.
Where did that family go?

And why am I
the only one
on this mantel?

There are probably digital pictures
     on Mom's old laptop
     but I need pictures I can take in
     and our printer's messed up.

I think I remember a box full of pictures—
     I guess no one around here
     was organized enough
     for photo albums.

The box was pretty
     with roses on the sides
     and it used to sit beside the rocker.

It's not there now.
     Missing, like the silver-framed
     family picture.

No family pictures
     on the family room walls.

Unless you count Shakespeare as family.
The kitchen has pictures of strawberries
        and blue dishes.
The hall has pictures of paths through woods.
The grown-ups in this family are missing.

There are just those old pictures of me.

And a space beside the rocker
        and on the mantel

    where a family used to be.

So now I have another question
     to ask Dad
     in the quiet of bedtime.

Not just
     Is that the same book
         in Mom's fairy tale?
but
     Where are the missing pictures?

I have another question
     that will only be asked
     in the quiet of my mind:

     If there are no family pictures

     does that mean
     there's no family?

Dad comes out of his study again

this time carrying his laptop.
I found some templates you can use
for the free kitten posters.

Why is he so eager
to make this house

emptier?

By bedtime
        I'm so worked up
        I almost don't even want
        to ask him anything. . . .
        Which question do I ask first?

I cuddle Serendipity
        and wait until he comes to say good night.
I wait until he straightens my covers.
I wait until he whisker-kisses my forehead . . .
        until he stands at the door

then I start with the easy one.
        Dad, that book you were reading today—
        what's it about?

Dad looks at his watch.
        It's a book of poems.

He hesitates at my pointed *And?*

That's a long story, Sara.
I'll tell you more about it later,
        all right? It's late. . . .

And now I can't ask
        my question about family pictures

        because how could that answer
        be a short story?

Our cottage
        is sweet in the daytime
        almost like a gingerbread house.

        Blooming vines climb
        the outside walls

        but they rustle against my window
        in the dark

                and I am afraid
                of their shadows

until
Serendipity appears.

It is hard
        to be afraid of the dark

        when a cat
                is standing on your face.

Dad doesn't have time this morning
　　　　to make scrambled eggs.

He tosses a Pop-Tart at me
　　　　clunks down a glass of orange juice
　　　　thwaps down a container of yogurt
　　　　slides a spoon across the table
　　　　　　　before I have a chance to move.

But what about Serendipity?
　　　　I ask.

He throws his head back
　　　　shoots air out of his mouth
　　　　then shoves a tiny bowl at me.
Run next door and ask for some cat food
　　　　he says.
We'll buy our own this afternoon.

I tuck my kitty into my sweater
　　　　race across wet grass in bare feet

and knock on Mrs. Whittier's door.

I see our reflection in the window.
    I haven't brushed my hair yet
    and it's sticking up wildly
    like Serendipity's head of fur.

We are dandelions of the morning.

Mrs. Whittier opens the door with a laugh
      and clasps her hands together.
      You have a kitty!

For now, I say.
      For a little bit, anyway.

She tilts her head
      sets her silver earrings swinging.
She may know more
      about my father and cats
      than she's ever let on.
You can tell me about it later—
      aren't you running late for school?

Yeah, I say, *but I need some breakfast*
      for Serendipity.

Named her already?
She takes the bowl
      and when she brings it back

Shoji—her tabby—is following her
his eyes on the bowl.

When she gives it to me
she reaches out the other hand
as if to smooth my hair
then draws it back
without touching me.

May you find a way to keep her, Sara.
Her solid voice has become soft.
If there's anything I can do. . . .

Miss Conglin looks up from her computer ·
       when I put my papers on her desk.
       Good to have you back, Sara
          she says with a smile.
       Did you understand all the makeup work?

I nod.

Did Garrett get the recording to you?

Yes. Thanks.
I wonder if I should say something more
       about the play

       and then three Lost Boys
       and Tiger Lily
       shove through the door
       with their furs and feathers
       all ready to be put away
       in the costume closet

and it seems like old news
that has nothing to do with
empty-handed
me.

I feel the Pan's presence
    when he enters the room.

    The performance has
    left its mark on him.

    A sixth-grade celebrity.

    The air tingles around him
    and when I look his way
    he's almost shiny.

I want to see the smile I saw
    at my door.
I want him to smile at me
    like when I was his Wendy.

But I can't even
    catch
    his
    eye.

Already I'm missing
        the feel of her in my arms.
Six hours is a long time to wait
        for a cuddle.
Six hours of clock-watching
        and busywork.
Six hours of hard chairs
        and hard pencils.
Six hours is too long
        without her.

What will I do
        if she has to go?

Kelli looks different today.
        She's sitting even straighter
        and tossing her shiny hair
        and laughing
        without covering her mouth.

I think that could be me
        if I were glowing from stardom

        but I feel pasty from the flu
        and I have nothing at school
        to laugh about.

Then Taylor raises her fingers at me
        like silly cat claws
        and she grins

        and laughter
        bubbles out of my body
        just as free and light
        as the ting-a-ling
        of a Tinker Bell chime.

Something has happened
        while I've been gone.
It seems to revolve around the thimble
        that Wendy gave Peter
        and Peter gave back—

        a substitute for a kiss.

There is a kind of energy
        in the classroom
        that has to do with giggling girls
        and oohing boys

        and thimbles appearing mysteriously
        on people's desks.

I'm not sure
        if the pretend kisses
        are real wishes
        or just teasing.

But I'm pretty sure

> I'm not a part
> of any of it
> anymore.

Garrett gets up to sharpen his pencil
       and I can't help but watch him.
       He moves so easily and confidently.

       Our Neverland time is over
       but yesterday's smile gave me hope
       for real time.

Now I'm not sure where
       that Garrett went.

I stare at the back of his head
       and wonder if his hair
       is as soft as my kitten's.

As he passes Kelli's desk
       his hand makes a quick movement
       and suddenly
       there is a folded triangle note
       in front of her.

What happened between my Peter Pan
            and the Wendy-imposter?

And if not for the flu

            would that note
            have been for me?

When I get home
> Serendipity is waiting for me
> in the window.

I open the door
> drop my backpack
> and give her a quick snuggle.

But something in the air
> is wrong.

No Dad-greeting.

I go through the house to find him.
He is in the kitchen
> kneeling in front of the potted tree
> digging in the dirt with an old spoon
> wearing a disgusted face.

What's wrong? I ask.

That cat, he says

    did her business in this pot.

The kitchen smells bad.

    Not like burned food

    or spoiled milk

    or rotten fruit . . .

    like bad kitten.

Now is definitely not the time
      to ask questions.
But I have to ask one eventually
      after the smell weakens.
      When are we going to buy cat food?

Dad raises his eyebrows at me.
      Do we really want
      to put anything more in
      now that we know what comes out?

Serendipity mews and I take a chance
      hold her up near his face
      and say in a kitty-voice
      Please feed me, kind sir.

Dad smiles with his eyes

      his mouth still holding
      those petrified tears.

We walk to the store
　　　like we walk everywhere.

　　　Dad hasn't replaced the car
　　　since The Accident.

Dad tells me I should
　　　bring along the posters
　　　to put up on the way.

　　　He mentions utility poles
　　　and bulletin boards
　　　at the used book store
　　　and the coffee hangout.

I tell him the posters
　　　aren't quite ready yet
　　　and I'll do it later
　　　with Taylor.

I'm beginning to think
    I really am a good actress
    because he buys it.

Aren't parents supposed to know
    when their kids are lying?

Dad and I slip silently past the stone dorm
    where Mom used to live.

    Two kittens
    are in one window

    looking like fuzzy slippers,
    the same as Serendipity.
    They must be the same age.

Once before when we saw
    a cat in a dorm window,
    Dad told me
    students aren't supposed
    to have pets in their rooms.

I have a funny feeling
       that is Jocelyn's window.

I see Dad notice the kittens,
       blink,
       and turn away

       like he hadn't seen
       Serendipity's family
       watching us walk by.

I see Taylor's mom
        in the cereal aisle
        and an awful scene
        begins to play in my mind.

Dad bringing up the kitten situation.
Taylor's mom knowing nothing about it.
Me—busted.
Taylor an accomplice.

Dad, I call
        pointing to something
        in the opposite direction
        like a cliché in a movie.

Dad looks at what I'm pointing to
        and so do I.
It's a tabloid with a headline about aliens
        and a fuzzy green impossible picture.

He looks at me with a question

etched in his face.
It's a where-did-I-go-wrong question
    a that-settles-it
        no-more-stupid-movies decision.

He's ready to lock me in my room
    with books, the old classics.

But it's okay.
Taylor's mom has left the building.

In the pet aisle
> Dad picks out
> the tiniest package of kitten food
> and a small bag of cat litter.

I almost point out
> the price-per-ounce difference
> in the bigger bags

> then I figure that might give away
> my plan for forever.

I reach for a blue litter box
> and Dad tells me
> *Put that back.*
> *We can make do with litter*
> *and a lined cardboard box*
> *for a week or less.*

I want to say
> *If you only knew. . . .*

But instead I joke
    The kitten's the one
    who's going to "make doo."
    Get it?

Dad just rolls his eyes
    and shakes his head.

Back at home, Dad tucks the kitten food
　　　　behind the fruit bowl on the counter
　　　　and notices Mrs. Whittier's soup pot
　　　　drying on the drainer.
　　　　Can you take this back
　　　　　　and thank her? A lot?

Sure, I say.
I pop Serendipity into the pot
　　　　and watch Dad's mouth drop open.
　　　　What could be cuter
　　　　than a kitten in a pot?

But Dad doesn't laugh or even smile.
He turns away.

A heartbeat later it occurs to me—
Mrs. Whittier has lived next door
　　　　all my life,
　　　　has been a big part of our lives
　　　　in the past.

She might know a lot
        she could tell me

        about family pictures
        and why our family
        doesn't look like a family

at all.

Mrs. Whittier takes the soup pot
    and croons at Serendipity.
Then she brushes aside my thanks.
    Of course, Sara.
    I just wish I could do more for you.

And so here is my chance.
    Do you think I could
        come in and talk?

Mrs. Whittier looks
    like I've handed her a gift.
    Yes, of course, come in.
    Tell me all about this little kitty.

I follow her and kitty-in-a-pot
    into the kitchen,
    explain how Serendipity
    was dropped off.

It's been a while since I've been in here

long enough that I don't recognize
her ceramic pieces displayed on the open shelf
or the bright woven tablecloth
that brushes my knees when I sit.

The usual smell of bread baking
has been replaced by something spicy.

I finish explaining and start to ask

but the question about family pictures
seems too heavy to lift.

I say instead, *Where are your kitties?*

Mrs. Whittier says, *Oh, you want to see them?*
She snaps her fingers in a repeating rhythm
  and Shoji and Kajiro come running
  the tabby a shadow
    to the orange and white Kajiro.

From under the tablecloth on my lap
  I hear hissing.
   Serendipity has become an air hose
    of noisy spitting.
   Shoji and Kajiro look up curiously.

Shouldn't they be the ones hissing? I ask.

Mrs. Whittier shakes her head.
  They're secure at home.
  She's the one who feels threatened.
She gives her cats a splash of milk in their bowls

as a reward for coming when called.

I lift the tablecloth to pet Serendipity
     and calm her down.
     She keeps spitting even though
     the cats have gone to their bowls.
     Why are you being so silly?

She'll be fine once you get her back home.

I put the tablecloth
     back over Serendipity's head.
     Only if I can keep her.

Mrs. Whittier smiles sadly.
     She looks down at her kitties
     and I notice they have
        new handmade bowls.
     How long has it been
        since I came to see her?

I'm suddenly ashamed.
Has Mrs. Whittier been as lonely as I have?

I try to remember who she has
    to keep her company at home
    besides her cats.

I know gentle Mr. Whittier died
    sometime after my mom.
Mrs. Whittier has a grown stepdaughter
    who was never very friendly

    but I don't think I've seen her
    since Mr. Whittier died.

I try to think of something to say
    to make up for not visiting all this time
    but no words come to me.

I thank her for the soup

    and make a run for it.

After dinner
>   Dad asks if I want
>   to look at The Book.
He seems resigned
>   to mentioning things
>   he'd rather not.

I think I've changed my mind.
>   I'm not sure I want to deal
>   with difficult things, either

>   not right now
>   when my visit with Mrs. Whittier
>   has made me realize
>   there are more empty spaces
>   in our lives now
>   than the space Mom left.

My excuses are pitiful.
>   *I just want a bath*

and to go to bed,
I say.
I'm so tired.

Dad looks surprised
but he nods.

I can feel him watching me
from the corners
of his eyes.

Tonight I discover
    a new form of marine life.

    It is white and fluffy
    and crouches on the edge of the tub.
        A *sea marshmallow.*

She wants to understand water.
        She sticks her tongue under the faucet.
        She watches the waves slosh
            when I scooch around.
        She waits for me to fill her up a cup.
        She likes to drink it warm.

She pats the bubbles.
She leans too far and falls in.

This is more about water
    than she wants to know.

I'm shocked enough
        by the sight of her
        struggling in the deep water
        that I yell   *Dad!*
I toss her out of the tub
        and hide behind
        the shower curtain.

He comes running
        but stops when he sees her,
        tufted legs splayed
        head down,
        miserable on the bath mat.

Stops and laughs.

She looks at him in reproach
        and shakes all over
        so hard she falls down.

Dad grabs a towel

and covers her in it
picks her up like a burrito baby
and roughs up her fur.

You goofy thing, he says.
How'd you get all wet?

She looks wide-eyed into his face
and reaches a sweet paw to his cheek.

Smart girl.

Tonight when Dad comes to say good night
    Serendipity is on my chest
    covered with my old baby blanket.

    The silky edges are frayed
    but the balloons make her look
    ready for a party.

He feels her around the ears.
    She's still a little wet, he says.
    Don't let her get you sick again.

She won't.   *She's nice and warm.*
Serendipity's head sticks out
    just barely from the blanket.
Look how cute she is, Dad.

He looks and his eyes go
    from soft to steely.
    He pins me with a stare
    and he shakes his finger.

Don't get any ideas.
I mean it, Sara.

What? I ask   innocently.

I hear the mumble of his voice
          as he leaves my room.
Don't give away your heart.

Dad trips over Serendipity three times
       while he's getting ready for work—
       coming out of the bathroom
       taking his shirt from the dryer
       moving breakfast to the table.

She has a way of getting under our feet
       like a sheepdog
              herding us toward her bowl
       or a miniature soccer player
              disrupting our goal.

I think it's funny.
Dad doesn't.

I catch him swearing once
       and I shake my finger at him.

       That is the wrong thing to do.

He narrows his eyes at me

and mutters, *Just a few more days.*

This makes him feel better.
It makes me feel awful.

Just a few more days
      is the worst curse of all.

I study my kitten posters on poles
    as I'm walking to school.

Taylor and I chose the poles
    where it would be hardest for Dad
    to see the phone numbers clearly
    on his regular route to class.

The changed phone numbers
    don't look too suspicious
    I hope.

I didn't make a picture
    of the cuteness of Serendipity.
    That wrong number would be getting
       too many calls.

I count the days—
    Today, Wednesday, Thursday, Friday.
    Will we get Saturday, too?
    Four or five days left

for Dad to fall in love
with this kitty.

We need to step up
the irresistible factor.

Quickly.

We're working on our Middle Ages unit
       and I'm not really listening
       because I can see Garrett
       out of the corner of my eye

       and in my mind
       he's wearing the armor of a knight.

My daydreaming is such a cliché.

Then Miss Conglin gets to Joan of Arc
       and my ears perk up.

       She was so brave and tragic.

Miss Conglin hasn't told us yet
       what the possibilities are
       for our character assignments.

       We will research and role-play
       the type of medieval person

we're given.

Before, I wanted to be royalty.
But now I think
Joan of Arc would be

the greatest role ever.

I must still be daydreaming because
　　　Miss Conglin says, *Sara*
　　　like she's already
　　　　　called my name before.

She's holding out a folded paper.
　　　It must be my character assignment.

I open it and read *Peasant*.

　　　It figures.

I glance over at Kelli
　　　who is beaming at her paper
　　　like someone who won the lottery.

　　　Kelli is probably a noble lady
　　　and she will ride off with Garrett
　　　on his steel-footed steed.

My kingdom for a horse.

That horse.
With Garrett on it.

I really need to give my mind
          something else to think about.

Thank goodness for Serendipity.

I find Taylor at the basketball court
        at recess.
I saw your mom
        at the grocery store yesterday
        I tell her.

Her face looks like—so what?
        Then she gets it
        and her lips get flat and long
        like when she's making a frog face.
Did your dad talk to my mom?

No. I kept him from seeing her.

Taylor bounces the basketball six times.
        Maybe I should say something to her
        just in case.

Like what?

She heaves the ball at the basket.

Like . . . Sara's got a kitten
she needs to find a home for.
You sure we can't have a kitten?

I nod.

Then at least she won't look clueless
if my dad says something to her.

This is getting too complicated.

I don't like this plot anymore.

After lunch, Miss Conglin says
>   *Remember, everyone—*
>   *tomorrow I want you to bring in*
>   *at least one picture*
>   *of life with your family.*
>   *We'll be using them as writing prompts*
>   *so having more might help*
>   *if you get stuck.*

I raise my hand.
>   *Do the pictures have to be recent?*

Miss Conglin shakes her head.
>   *No, the age of the photos*
>   *doesn't matter.*

I feel like she's purposely
>   keeping the compassion
>   off her face.

>   Like maybe she knows

I wish my family
was normal.

I remember Peter Pan saying,
Don't have a mother.
And me telling him,
O Peter,
no wonder you were crying.

I am not going to ask him.

I should not have to ask my father
        where there are pictures
        of my own family.

I should not have to ask him
        why there is no visible evidence
        our family ever existed.

No.   I will find them on my own
        if they are there to be found.

I am not going to beg.
I am not going to plead.

I am not going to do anything
        to make him
                almost

                        cry.

I sneak in the house
        grab up Serendipity
        and let her climb on my shoulder.
I drop my backpack in the corner
        and head out the door.

Mrs. Whittier's is the best place
        I can think of
        to unearth family secrets.

I will pretend
        our last conversation
        was easy.

I will pretend
        I never drifted away
        from Mrs. Whittier's life.

I am pretty sure
        she has forgiven me.

So we will begin again.
Clean slate.

I knock.
She opens the door wide
  gauze sleeves fluttering in welcome.

I step inside quickly.
  What can you tell me
  about after?

Her mouth opens
　　　　but no sound comes out.
Then, *After what, Sara?*

I heave a sigh.
　　　　I need a family picture for school.
　　　　I can't find any.
　　　　They're all missing.
Serendipity creeps beneath my hair
　　　　and I put a steadying hand on her.
　　　　Do you know
　　　　what happened to us
　　　　after . . . my mom died?

Mrs. Whittier stretches her arms to me
　　　　then pulls them back
　　　　then looks at her ceramic-rough hands
　　　　as if willing them to move.

　　　　She sits down on her couch

and pats the leaf-print cushion beside her
then pats my knee as I sit.

I haven't gotten to hug you for years,
        she says.
Do you remember when you used to
        lean against me to get a hug?

I shake my head.

Mrs. Whittier says,
        When your mother died
        all four of your grandparents came.
        You were surrounded by family. . . .
She reaches up to scratch Serendipity
        under her chin and jaw.
        I thought you'd be okay.
Serendipity leans into her fingers
        claws tightening on my shoulder.
        But when they left
        your dad retreated into himself
        and he took you with him.
Mrs. Whittier stops petting Serendipity
        and turns her clear eyes full on me.

Maybe I should have done something sooner.
But I thought you two just needed time
  to lift out of it.
But your dad has never smiled much again
and you . . .
you just disappeared into . . .

She stops.

Into what? I ask.

I don't know.
  Into his sadness?
She shakes her head.
  It would break your mother's heart
  to see you both like this.

Mrs. Whittier bumps me with her elbow.

 Remember how she used to sing
 "Put on a Happy Face"?
 With that cheesy tap dance?
 She loved to see you smile.

She teases another memory

 from way back in my mind—
 sunlight bouncing off Mom's bright hair
 as Mom leads me to a backyard room
 she made from branches
 wound with flowers and floaty scarves.

Mrs. Whittier remembers it, too.

 You called it your fairy castle.

In my mind, I see a pitcher of lemonade

 in Mom's hands.
 She let me pick blossoms
 for the fairies' cups.

Of course, Mrs. Whittier says.
    Your mother got such a kick
    out of your imagination.

Serendipity jumps off my shoulder
        and into her lap
        begging for attention.

Yes, yes, Mrs. Whittier baby-talks to her.
        She would get a kick out of you, too.

I wonder if she is just
       making small-talk.
       Would she really?

Are you kidding?
Your mother would have loved
       this little kitty, Mrs. Whittier says.

I sit quietly
       heart beating loudly.
       Then why? I ask.
       Why did we never get a cat?

Mrs. Whittier looks like someone
       who has just said too much.
       Cornered.
       Shifty-eyed.
She shakes her head.
       I'm sorry, Sara.
       That's something you'll need

to ask your dad.

I consider stomping off in a huff
        but then I won't get to talk
        about Mom.

And I need this.

Maybe Mrs. Whittier is thinking
      about what I'd face
           if I asked Dad.
      I remember once
      when your dad was grumpy
      from grading papers . . .

At the sound of her sudden laughter
      Shoji's and Kajiro's heads pop up
      from where the cats are curled
      hidden behind a trailing vine.

      Mrs. Whittier's plants look like
      she can never bear to trim them.
      They sprawl like
      cats outside on a warm day.

She got you and herself
      dressed up in fifties-style clothes
      and turned on that song from Grease.
She wipes a tear off her laughter.

That one at the end.
And you two danced and sang
on the back deck
for your daddy.

What did he do? I ask.

Don't you remember?
Matthew smiled so big
he looked like his face would crack.

She tells Mom stories
> until my insides feel satisfied
> like eating baked potato soup
> on a cold night.

About the pictures . . .
> I ask finally.
Where do you think they are?

Mrs. Whittier shrugs.
> *I'm guessing your dad*
> *has them somewhere close*
> *but not out where*
> *he has to see them*
> *all the time.*

I take a deep breath.
> *I'm going to find them.*

I'm almost daring her to stop me.

She looks at me steadily
     then holds out her arms

     and I lean into her.

I think I remember this
     after all. . . .

I make my hands like a leash
     around Serendipity's tummy
     lean over and let her feel
          the grass under her toes.

     I'm planning my search
     as we make our way
     slowly back to the house.

It would be easiest to tell Dad
     I need a family picture

     but I want more than that.

I want to see them all.

So when he calls out,
     I have office hours.
     See you at five thirty.
     Mrs. Whittier is on standby,

I make my move
at the sound of the door closing.

His room is his sanctuary
so I start there
in the forest green gloom.
I search under the unmade bed
in his messy drawers
in his closet that twangs
with unused hangers

and behind the abandoned tennis racquets
I find the box stashed way in back.

Treasure.

My hands start to shake
      so I can barely lift the box.
I take it back to my room.
I don't want to be caught
      with the rose-covered box
      in his dark room.

I close my door.
I lift the lid.
I start to cry.

We were a family once.
Here is the proof I remember—
      Mom with a garland of flowers in her hair
            gazing up at Dad
              in their wedding photo.
      Sun-soft Mom cradling baby me.
      Bright-eyed Dad with toddler me
            on his shoulders.
      So many smiles.

I can't stop looking.

I hear Dad come into the house.
        My alibi is ready.
        I needed it for school.

But he doesn't come to my room.

I decide I will hide the box here
        so I can keep looking.

Dad has dinner ready
        soon after he gets home.

When he calls
        I pluck out one picture
        and shove the box
        in my closet

        almost a mirror
        of where he'd hidden it.

I hear a bump behind me
        and back out quick
        heart thumping

        but it was only Serendipity
        knocking three paperbacks
        off my bookshelf.

I slip the picture
        into my social studies book.

King Tut looks at me
from the cover
slyly keeping mum.

Our family is finally
out of the box

ready to see the world.

I open a new milk jug
          to pour our drinks for dinner.

The plastic ring that sealed the lid
          pops off and rolls on the ground

          a sudden thrill for Serendipity.

She chases
          she pounces
                    she swats and sends it flying.
She races
          she bounces
                    she puts on a tumbling show.

After a while she calms down
          picks up the circle in her teeth
                    and carries it off.

I look at Dad

to see his reaction.

He has just turned back to the stove
      but not quickly enough to hide it:

    a tiny grin tilting
          the corner of his mouth.

Dad puts the pot of tomato soup
in the middle of the table
with a plate of grilled cheese sandwiches.

While he ladles the soup into our bowls
I consider.
I'm torn between asking
once and for all
why no cats are allowed

torn between that
and getting Dad to fall in love
with Serendipity.

I decide it's smarter
to go with love.

Serendipity is intrigued
by the smell of cheese
and jumps onto an empty chair

then onto the table.

Plan already foiled.

Dad stands to grab the kitten
            but she freaks at his sudden move
            and tears off the table
            and out of the room.

Dad just looks at me

            and shakes his head.

Luckily it's my turn
       to do the dishes.

I'm right near the phone when it rings.

The voice is tentative.
       You don't by any chance
       have a kitten
       you're trying to get rid of,
       do you?

I'm not lying when I say No.

Sorry.   *I saw this flyer and called*
       and the number on it was wrong
       and I thought maybe I saw where
       the mistake was. . . .

She apologizes again

and I say it's all right.

But it's not.

What if someone else
        is smart enough to figure it out
        and Dad answers?

Dad calls from his study.
        Who was that?

Just Taylor, I lie.

Bedtime has become
        much more fun
        since Serendipity arrived.

She thinks my feet
        are small animals
        burrowing under the covers
                like moles under the lawn.

It is her job
        to stop the moles
        to pounce on the moles
        to wrestle the moles
        until
        they are too afraid
                to move.

She does her job well.

Miss Conglin tells us to put our photos
          at the top of our desks.
Before we start writing
          she lets us walk around
          and see everyone else's pictures.

Garrett's family must like camping.
          He and his little sisters and parents
          are messing around in front of a tent.

Walking further
          I see I am not the only one
          with a broken family.

I forgot how Breanna lives alone
          with her grandmother.

Giselle's pictures
          show two different houses
                    her mom in one

her dad in the other.

Jaime has a shot
of him and his dad
before his dad was deported.

I guess all families
have some kind of story.

In my chosen picture
      my parents sit on a piano bench
      with little me on Mom's lap.

It looks like Easter.

We're all dressed up
      and I'm holding a basket.

      One of my legs
      is flung off to the side
      like I can't wait to get down
      and find those hidden eggs.

Mom's arms surround me
      like she's holding
      something precious.

Dad's face shines with twinkling eyes
      and a crooked grin.

I glance over at my picture
from across the room.

It seems to glow with the promise
of a story

but I'm not looking for a story prompt

I'm looking for something else

and I'm not sure what it is.

After we've walked around the room
        we head back to our desks
        to begin working.

I see Garrett stop at Kelli's desk
        and hear them laughing
        about a bulldog in Kelli's picture
        dressed up like a pirate.

Something in me sinks.

I wonder if Garrett knows the dog.
I wonder if Garrett has been to Kelli's house
        like he's been to mine

        only not just there
        to drop off something
                from the teacher.

        There because he wanted to be.

Maybe Garrett feels me watching him
because he looks over at me

and smiles.

Oh.

Does he know I like him?

Is he throwing me a crumb?

I look down at my happy picture
        but it makes me sad.

I begin writing without thinking.

Once upon a time there was a family.
Then there was none.
Once upon a time there was a mom
who lived and breathed and danced and sang

who loved and dreamed and wished on stars.

Then there was a car.
Then there was a fog.
Then there was the sound of metal
and it was not the sound
of swords and armor
in a story about Joan of Arc
but the crash of a car
as the fog stole the mother's sight

and the headlights of eighty other cars
that piled up like broken sticks
beneath a burning stake.

Once upon a time there was a family.
Then there was none.

I didn't realize a picture
　　of a bright Easter morning
　　could prompt such dark writing.

I feel like I just burped
　　a cloud of smoke.

A hand appears near my picture.
　　A finger points to Mom.

　　Garrett on his way to the front.

　　He lifts a strand of my hair
　　that's close to my cheek.
　　Two blondies, he says.
　　You look just like her.

I stop breathing a moment
　　as the sun comes out
　　from behind a thick cloud.

Wondering how I should react
to his touch
and his words.

She looks beautiful in the picture
to me.

Is that how I look
to him?

Walking home from school
      I pass Mom's dorm.
The kittens are in the window again.
On an impulse, I climb over bushes
      to tap-play with them
      on the glass.
But the kittens startle at me coming so close
      and one falls into the room.

The curtain moves and reveals Jocelyn
      who widens her dark-fringed eyes.
She pulls open the window.
Sara! How are you?

Good. I motion through the window opening.
      I was just gonna look at the kittens.

I figured.   *How's your new kitty?*

I blink.   I guess she's not keeping secrets.

Great—well—I don't know
if I'll be able to keep her.

She makes an exaggerated frowny face.
Fingers crossed, right?

Right.

Jocelyn looks back into the room
then says . *As long as you're here . . .*

Why don't you stay and talk awhile, she says.
Climb on in.

I don't know what my dad
      would think about this
      but I climb in anyway
      twisting past a scrambled desktop
      trying not to disturb a long-legged girl
         sprawled on the opposite bed.
The kittens scatter when I land.
      Where'd you get these kittens?

Their mom was a stray . . . pregnant.
      She got hit by a car after they were born.
      We're still trying to find homes
         for these last two.
Jocelyn waits a beat and
      gives me a considering look.
Do you know if your mom lived here?

I nod.   *Yeah, this was her dorm.*

I thought so.   When I heard your fairy tale
      and I saw her name, Aislinn,
      I wondered if it was the same one.
      That's an unusual name.

The leggy girl sits up.
      Jocelyn. That's not for outsiders.

Jocelyn shrugs.
      She's not really an outsider.
She turns back to me.
      She left an artifact.

My mind goes to old pottery and arrowheads.
      Artifact?

Come on, I'll show you.

Jocelyn leads me across the hall
      to another dorm room.
      Coming through

she says to the occupants.
This is Sara.
Aislinn's daughter.

The girls look up from their books
    and gaze at me.
It makes me feel like a zoo creature.

Jocelyn twists a lamp
    so that it shines into a drawer.

    She pushes aside pens,
    index cards, and highlighters.
    Take a peek, she says to me.

The inside of the drawer is littered
      with graffiti.
      Dorm tradition, Jocelyn says.
      Girls who get engaged
      while they're here
      put their names in the drawer.

I follow her finger
      to my mother's name.
      She's written
      Aislinn and Matthew.

Jocelyn sighs.
      Isn't it romantic?

She leans toward me.
      Your parents must have been
      secretly engaged.
      It's against the rules
      for a professor and a student

to have a relationship.
She leans back.
 But how can love be
  against the rules?
She shakes her head
 at how ridiculous that sounds.

Jocelyn jumps up all of the sudden.
 Omigosh, I'm late for a test.
She gathers notebooks and pens.
 Don't worry about that rule thing.
 It was a long time ago.
 Things worked out—right?
She flashes me a counselor's smile.
 Gotta run!

She's gone just like that
 and I feel dumb with these girls
  I don't know
 so I drift back across the hall
 half-smile at the girl on the bed
 and scramble out the window

 heading for home

and that rule-breaker—
my dad.

I guess I'm not the only one
who's wanted something
not allowed.

Walking home
	I almost kick myself.
	I could have at least petted the kittens.

Fortunately, I still have my own at home.

Serendipity follows me into the living room
	grabbing at my shoelaces.

There's an empty spot on the bookshelf
	where The Book was.

Dad comes around the corner
	his arms full of sheets
	his face full of disgust.
It's hard to imagine him
	as the rebellious romantic hero.
	Guess where the little monster
	decided to pee		he says.

Um   Uh-oh.   *Your bed?*

Righto.   Heavy sigh.
Any phone calls yet?
        Or what about Taylor's mom?

Dad, I say
        and then I stop.

What else can I say?

I follow Dad to the washing machine.
Maybe you could teach me to do laundry
      I say.

He gives me a double take.
      Why the sudden interest?

I put Serendipity on the dryer
      to let her peek into the washer.
      So if this happens again
      I could fix it instead of you.

Dad narrows his eyes
      shows me which way
      to turn the knobs
      and twist the dial,
      how much detergent to put in.

Then he says
      It's not like she'll be here long enough

to make this a habit.
Saturday morning at the latest.

I clutch her like a baby
        stunned by the real time frame
        and scratch her forehead.
        No, I know
        I say.

But I'm hoping I don't.

Serendipity tries to help us make up the bed
        by standing in the middle of the mattress
        paws reaching as the sheet floats down.
        She dances out of our reach.

Finally Dad says, *Just grab her*
        and I'll do this myself.

I tackle her and pluck her claw-hold
                from the mattress.
        I sit in the armchair
                and hold her on my lap
                so she looks like she's sitting
                like a regular person.

Dad, I say
        to get his attention.

He turns to look
        and I hear his breath go in sharp
        at the sight of us.

He quick-flips the covers
>at the end of the bed
>and the *Love Songs* book
>goes flying toward the dresser.

Dad sees me looking at it.
He picks it up
>and puts it on his nightstand.

I think he's going to say something
>but he doesn't.

With his chin, he holds a pillow
>ready to drop
>into an opened pillowcase.

Dad, I say.

He lets the pillow fall into the case.
>Sighs.
Your mom gave me that book
>*to let me know how she felt about me.*

So—what's the long story?

He reaches for the book.
>Cradles it in both hands.
>Silent.

Dad, I say, *I want to talk about her sometimes.*
>*Couldn't we   talk about her?*

He replaces the book.
>His hands drop to his sides.

Serendipity must think
>there's a treat in his hand
>because she springs from my lap
>and claws her way up his pant leg
>to investigate.

Dad yells and pulls her off
>like she's a sticky burr.
He tosses her onto the bed.
That's enough for now.

He's looking at Serendipity
>but I'm pretty sure
>>he's talking to me.

I pick up Serendipity
    and take her from his room.

I go into my room and close the door.
Not sure what to do now.

I stand by the door and
    watch Serendipity play hide-and-seek
    with my blankets and quilt.

I can hear Dad finishing up his bed
    then footsteps to his study
    then outside my door.

I wait on my side of the door
    feeling kind of ridiculous.

Serendipity runs to the door
    and paws at it.

A good excuse to open it.

Dad's there

     looking like he got caught

     doing something he shouldn't.

     Looking like he feels silly.

Then he holds out the book

     and a piece of paper.

Here, he says.
>   *I know I should be able to*
>   *talk about her with you*
>   *but I just can't.*
>   *Not yet.*

I take the book
>   and the paper
>   from his trembling hands.

He turns to go
>   then turns back.
He taps the book.
>   *Mom named you*
>   *after how we began . . .*
>   *with Sara's poems.*

He doesn't stay
>   to watch me read them.

It's a really old book.

> *Love Songs*, by Sara Teasdale.

I wonder if this is a poet

> Dad teaches about

> in his American Lit class.

Inside the front cover

> there's an inscription—

> For Matthew,

>> who makes the world

>> a poem.

Then the book flips open

> to a poem called "The Look"

> like it's been opened

> to this page

> time after time.

Someone has pasted in

> the name "Matthew"

over one of the original names.

It had to be Mom.

Now with Mom's editing
     the poem says,

       "Strephon kissed me in the spring,
       Robin in the fall,
       But Matthew only looked at me
       And never kissed at all.

       "Strephon's kiss was lost in jest,
       Robin's lost in play,
       But the kiss in Matthew's eyes
       Haunts me night and day."

It's like another artifact
        Mom left behind.
An arrowhead from Cupid.

How did Mom have the nerve
        to give her professor
        a book like this?

He couldn't help but get the message
        loud and clear.

She put it all out there.
I think of Garret and wonder
        if I'll ever be able to do that.

Many of these are not happy poems.
A lot are about death.
I don't know how Dad can bear
        to read this one:

"I SHALL NOT CARE

"When I am dead and over me bright April
    Shakes out her rain-drenched hair,
Though you should lean above me broken-
       hearted,
    I shall not care.

"I shall have peace, as leafy trees are peaceful
    When rain bends down the bough,
And I shall be more silent and cold-hearted
    Than you are now."

No wonder my dad
    has such a hard time

      smiling.

I put the book down
　　　lift Serendipity off my legs
　　　and go to my closet.

I want to see more family pictures
　　　so I can follow where this story went.
　　　How the two of them
　　　became the three of us.

This time I upend the box
　　　and spread the pictures out
　　　like I'm playing with money.

And a patch of orange
　　　catches my eye.

A cat sitting like a little person
　　　on Mom's lap.

I never knew she had a cat.

I look through other pictures in that area
  and find a bunch more
  of an orange cat
  with a tail like a flame.

And pictures of the cat and me
  from baby to toddler.

    Orange cat touching its nose to mine.
    Orange cat leaping into my lap
      on the rocking chair.
    Orange cat cuddled against my stomach
      as we nap on the floor of the den.

No wonder I love cats.

In the last one I find, I'm a tiny baby.

    I'm lying on our blue couch

with the cat on the back of it
looking down at me.

I wish I could remember looking up
and seeing that furry face.

I wish I knew why
a cat was okay before
and it's not okay now.

I think Serendipity
        slept on my head last night.
I can feel puncture marks
        in my scalp
        where she kneaded herself
        to sleep.

Stayed up way too late
        for a Wednesday night
        reading most of *Love Songs*
        and looking at pictures.

Half-asleep
        I step on a piece of paper
        and almost fall over
        trying to unstick it from my foot.

Oh.

It's the paper Dad gave me last night.
        I fell asleep and forgot about this.

I should be getting ready for school

but I have to stop and read it.

SMALL DEMANDS

For two days now
the child has appeared
when I've reached the best part of a novel.
She places herself between me and the words
her chubby hand planted on the page
like a bagel with fingers. . . .
The bagel will not be removed.
I try lifting it gently, at first,
then I grasp her wrist
then I pry at her palm
but she quickly frees herself
and slaps her heavy hand back on the resolution.

It will have to wait.

She senses I have given in
and settles sweetly into my lap
pointing to numbers on the page

and reciting them.
She turns pages and asks for words
eyes bright with my attention
fingers light with learning.

Every cat I've owned has refused to budge
from a newspaper spread out on the floor
in front of an anxious reader.
But cats can be shut behind doors.

I have a child.
The story will wait.

She loved me.

I mean, I knew that
  and I felt that
  and I remembered that.

But here is more evidence

  and at the same time
  I'm teary with love
  I'm angry with Dad.

Why didn't he give this to me sooner?

Why is he so wrapped up
  in his stupid grief

  that he won't let me
  have my own?

I am storming out of my room
     with cat pictures
     and the poem
     when my foot kicks
     the *Love Songs* book.

I honestly need to stop
     dropping things on the floor.

I pick up the book
     and like black-light lit fingerprints
     I can see Dad's tenderness
     all over it.

The book
     melts me
     toward Dad.

Less stormy now
     I take the pile of artifacts

to the kitchen.

Dad has toasted me a waffle
     and cut me a grapefruit
     and is heading out the door
     with his leather schoolbag
     and a backward wave.

Wind out of my sails.

Before I leave for school
   I go into Dad's room
   with evidence.
I want it to stand out
   so I make his bed.

I wonder if I should put the lone pillow
   in the middle at the top   ·
   even though he still sleeps
   only on his own side.
Maybe this is why
   he never makes his bed.

I place his pillow on his side   ·
   and center a picture
   on the pillow.

The picture is of me—
   baby on a blue couch

with a furry guardian angel.

He'll wonder how I got the picture.

I wonder if he'll be mad.

But he'll know
    that I know

    cats were not always
    forbidden.

It seems pointless
        to hide the pictures now.
I leave the pile in the middle of my floor
        and close my door
        against Serendipity
        so she can't ruin them.

I have one picture
        in my sweatshirt pocket
        to have it near me.

It's of me and the orange cat
        looking out the front window
        along with a reflection of my mom
        taking the picture.

I wave good-bye to Serendipity
        looking out the same window.

Mrs. Whittier is in her front yard

doing something with flowers.
I jog over to her.

Good morning, Sara!

I know something   I tell her.
    I pull out the picture
    and show it to her.
But Dad's still not talking.

Mrs. Whittier nods gently.

I turn and head for school.

Miss Conglin tries to relate
        subject matter to our lives.
So she brings back the thimble kiss.

A metaphor, she says during writing time,
        uses one word to stand for another.
She steps forward
        grabs the thimble off of Ana's desk
        and holds it up.
Just like Wendy, some of you in class
        have been using a thimble
        to represent a kiss.
She holds up her hand
        against the outburst of silliness.
You've been using a metaphor.

Well   I haven't used this metaphor,
        because I am thimble-less.

I glance at Garrett
        off to my left.

He is doing some kind of magic trick
        where he can make his thimble
        disappear and reappear.

No one's listening to Miss Conglin
        who's moved on to similes.

Our minds are on metaphors.

Taylor has a peasant assignment like me
     so we research together in class.

I slide the picture out of my pocket
     and show it to Taylor.
     Notice anything off in this picture?

She takes the close-up
     and says   *Ha   look at that.*
     A cat.
     I thought cats weren't allowed.

     I thought so, too, I say.
     My dad's got some explaining to do.

Taylor hands me back the picture.
     New plan?

I don't know.

I'm just winging it
right now.

She taps her pencil on her notebook
    ticking down the minutes.
    Time's running out   she says.

Believe me—
    I don't need reminding.

Sitting too long is hard for Taylor.
When Miss Conglin is busy,
        her back turned,
        Taylor stands up
                and holding the page
                she's been working on
                in one hand
        she does a mini peasant
        dance and song.

I have no soap
My bed is hard
My bread is smeared
with greasy lard
I have no bath
I'm full of fleas
Someone, won't you
help me, please

Something nags at my mind

as I'm laughing.
Hey, Taylor, do you know
    any of the songs from Grease?

Taylor shoves me.
    That's not the kind of grease
    I was singing about.
    But yeah   *I know them all.*

I tell her why I want to know
    and she says
    Come over after school.
    I've got the DVD.

Taylor's house is the opposite of mine.
There is honest-to-goodness life here.

First we visit
        the chickens and ducks in the coop
        and the bunnies in their cages.
Then Taylor lifts Mandy
        by an arm and an ankle
        and swings her around like an airplane.
Then Taylor's mom gives us cookies
        fresh from the oven.
Then we dance like hooligans
        in the family room
        to the great songs from *Grease*.

It's awesome.

Until we get to the end of the last song
        the one Mom and I sang for Dad.

I can't believe the lyrics.

The happy crowd is singing
We'll always be together
on and on and on.

Taylor notices I've stopped dancing
and I see the moment when she gets it
in a ripple across her face.
Um, you want to go outside
and hug a bunny?

Yes.   I do.
And then I want to go home
to Serendipity.

I'm at my front door
     when I hear Mrs. Whittier calling.

Sara,   *wait.*

Serendipity has already seen me
     from her spot in the window.
     Her mouth opens in silent mews.
I put my hand on the glass and tell her
     Just a minute, Dipity.

Mrs. Whittier is holding a CD.
     My stepdaughter's
          finally coming to visit.
     I found this while I was
     cleaning out the guest room.

I probably look as clueless as I feel.

When you were little
     and I sat for you at night

I'd play this CD
your mom made you for bedtime—
it's her voice telling you fairy tales.

I feel a tickle of a memory.

Mrs. Whittier twists her mouth around.
  I shouldn't be the one telling you this
  but you know about the cat now
  and Matthew can't seem
  to talk about it.

I have no idea what that
  has to do with fairy tales.

Then she tells me how the cat died
  because they didn't notice an infection
  until it was too late

  and how guilty Mom felt about it

  and how she cried for three days.

That was the cause for no more cats.

And when I got old enough to start asking
for a cat of my own
that was the reason the cat pictures
were hidden.
That was the reason one fairy tale
could not be played
and why it was removed from the book.

They didn't want me to think
cats were a possibility in this house.

Wait I say *What good would that do
if I already knew about the cat?*

Mrs. Whittier shakes her head.
You were two when that kitty died.
You'd forgotten about him by the time
you asked for a cat.

She hands me the CD.
The cat fairy tale is the first one.

I can't believe I'm holding
 Mom's voice in my hand.

Go on, now Mrs. Whittier says with a smile.
 You know you want to.

I make a dash for my CD player
 grabbing up Serendipity on the way.

Dad is still safely at school.

I drop in the disk
 and settle us on my bed
  my kitty curled in the center
  of my crisscrossed legs.
All I have to do
 is push the button
 to hear my mom's voice.

I'm almost afraid to do it.

Listen, Serendipity.
This is my mom.

Mom's voice tears my heart
    when she starts.
    Okay, honey bunny,
        snuggle down.
        Here's your story.

Once upon a time a princess lived in an ivy-covered tower. The tower walls were hard, cold stone. From her window she could see a meadow where furry creatures played in the sun, and she longed to cuddle their warm, soft bodies. But the rule-keepers had forbidden animals. No creatures were allowed inside to comfort her.

The princess was lonely.

One night, she heard a cry from below. She tiptoed down the stone staircase to find out who made the sound. She peeked outside the door into the dark. At first, she saw nothing. There was no one on the doorstep. The bushes held their secrets. The princess called out into the night, "Someone, someone who is scared, I am here. Come to me."

The bushes trembled and rustled and frightened the princess. But she remembered she was lonely and she became brave again.

She called, "Someone, someone who is scared, I am here. Come to me."

And this time the bushes answered her with a quavering mew, and a furry creature tumbled out and poked a nose at her outstretched hand. He twined his tiny body around her ankles until she picked him up and held him in her arms.

She remembered the rules about creatures. But the kitten creature was scared and alone and she was brave and alone. So she brought the kitten to her tower room and kept him there. And they were happy.

But it wasn't long until the rule-keepers heard about the kitten and demanded she turn him out. The princess couldn't bear to lose the kitten. So she wove a magic rune, a spell to make him invisible.

This worked for a while. But the kitten was playful. One day he saw the rune beckoning like a string and he pounced on it. He worried it until the rune unwound and floated out the window. It landed on the shoulder of a rule-keeper, who looked up to see where the rune had come from. He saw the kitten in the window.

At the same time, the princess noticed the kitten was no longer cloaked by the rune. She ran to get the kitten out of sight and looked out the window to make sure no one had seen. Below was the rule-keeper, watching. The princess didn't notice he was smiling. She only knew he had seen the forbidden kitten. Thinking all was lost, she fainted.

When the rule-keeper saw the princess faint, he rushed into the tower and up the stone stairs. He cradled the lonely princess in his arms and murmured comforting words to the kitten. When the princess awoke she was overwhelmed by his tenderness. The rule-keeper in turn was captivated by her heart. He invited the princess and her kitten to live in his warm cottage where there were no rules against furry creatures. The princess and the kitten joyfully accepted his invitation.

And they all lived in the cottage happily ever after.

Now close your eyes, honey bunny
and dream of sweet things.

I am full
    with the sound
    of Mom's voice.

But in the silence that comes
    with the ending of her story
    I have this thought—
        The rules are back . . .

    and I hear a noise.

I glance toward my open door
    and catch a glimpse
    of Dad turning away

    catch an echo
    of Dad retreating
    once again
    to his room.

How much did he hear?

It wouldn't matter.

He could fill in the gaps
     of his own story
     told in the voice
     of his dead wife.

I should have closed the door.

Now I regret
 leaving the picture
 of me and the orange kitty
 in his room.

He will go in there
 with her voice in his head

 and see evidence
 of my prying and accusing.

He may never want to talk to me again.

I want to go to his door
 and test this out.

I want to hear him say
 he loves me anyway.

I am too afraid to ask.

Dinner is saved
　　　because he has his phone
　　　in his room.

I wondered what we'd do for dinner
　　　if he never came out

　　　but he has solved that problem.

The pizza guy rings the doorbell
　　　and Dad opens his door
　　　a slit.

Use the money in the jar, Sara.
　　　I'm not feeling well.
　　　Help yourself.

That's usually a phrase directing you
　　　to serve yourself some food.

But this time, it feels wider:

Help yourself, Sara
because Dad
can't help you now.

The pizza
usually a happy food
tastes hard
and uncaring.

After pizza
    I drift back to my room.

Dad's door is still closed.

I'd like to hear Mom's voice again
    but I'm afraid Dad will hear
    even through closed doors.

I pick up *Love Songs*.
There are a few poems at the end
    I never got to
    so I read them now.

And the last one I hear in Mom's voice.
I can remember her reading this to me
    many times.
Maybe it was her favorite.

Here is the best line:
    "I think that every path we ever took

Has marked our footprints in mysterious fire,
Delicate gold that only fairies see."

She made magic for me.
I don't want that to end.

For no good reason other than
      I'm just sick of this sad house—
      I desperately want to storm
      the prince's castle.

      But I've already burned
         that drawbridge.

Serendipity leaps from nowhere and lands
      on the open pages of *Love Songs*
      pressing claw marks into the paper.
I gasp and push her away   *No!*

She looks surprised and scared
      and I suddenly remember . . .

Tomorrow is my only day left
      to woo the prince

      and he's locked up in his room.

*   ❁   *

It occurs to me as I'm walking
        lonely to school . . .

        if Dad doesn't fall in love by tonight—
        by tomorrow morning
        Serendipity will be on her way
        to the shelter.

That was the deal.
Well, Dad didn't know about
        the falling in love part

        but as far as he's concerned
        today is my last chance
        to find her
        a home somewhere else.

I am past panicking about losing her
        and starting to realize

        I could be responsible for

letting her end up
　　at the shelter.

She might die because
　　I brushed off a phone call.

And it will be my turn
　　to cry nonstop.

Miss Conglin announces a special treat.
>   We will watch a DVD this afternoon—
>   our production of *Peter Pan*.
She's brought popcorn
>   and pillows for us to sit upon
>   on the floor.

This day just keeps getting worse.
>   Serendipity is in peril
>   and now I'll have to sit through
>   that whole painful performance.

I'm moaning to Taylor at recess
>   and Kelli hears me.
>   She swishes by and says
>   *Too bad you missed it, Sara.*

Not too bad for you
>   I throw back at her.
It's supposed to sound like a joke
>   but I get my voice wrong.

It sounds like an accusation
      like my words are pointing fingers.
      I can feel the just-kidding look
      fall off my face.
So I say it instead:
      I'm just kidding.
      Really.

But I sound like a mean girl.

Kelli flips back
> *What's wrong with you?*
> *You won anyway.*

I have no idea what she's talking about.

I turn to Taylor and she looks
> as confused as I do.

Taylor gets her Harriet-the-Spy look
> and says, *I'm on it.*

She casually walks over to
> a group of Kelli's friends.

She's back in no time.
> *Remember that note you told me*
> *Garrett gave to Kelli?*

I nod.

He was answering her do-you-like-me note.

He checked "I like someone else."

Hope flares.

He didn't say,
*   but they think it's you.*

Maybe this day isn't so bad
     after all.

Garrett sits in the second row of pillows
       and there is an empty pillow
       in front of him.

I don't wait for someone else to sit there.
I remember how my mom
       made things happen
       and I think maybe
       I can do that too.

I try to be casual.
       I sit in front of Garrett
       like I don't notice he's there.
       I can see his straggling foot
       out of the corner of my eye.

I put my hands behind me
       like I'm going to lean back
       and my fingers brush his shoe.

He jerks it back.

I look behind me   grin.
          Foot still ticklish?

And then I see that slow smile come
          like a sunrise on a lake.

Beautiful.
Too bad I have to face forward.

I decide the best way
        to get through this performance
        is to imagine myself
        in the role.

I manage it all the way to the end
        when Wendy is grown up
        and her daughter says of Peter
        He does so need a mother.

And Wendy says, *Yes, I know.*
        No one knows it so well as I.

Just then a piece of popcorn
        sails over my head
        and lands in my lap.

I look behind me at Garrett
        mock-studying the ceiling

with a smile twitching
at the edges of his lips.

He's underlining the end.

Because there on the screen
        is the whole cast
        taking in applause and
        holding up a big sign that says
                For Sara!

That image warms me
      as I'm walking home from school.
      It overlays a cold feeling.
      How can I get Dad
      to fall in love with Serendipity?

Maybe I could soften him up.
I try to remember what kinds of things
      used to make Dad happy.
I flash on pictures from the box
      where we're hiking in Yosemite.
      He loved walking through the trees.

We haven't done any hiking
      since Mom died.
We don't even have a car to get us there.
But he does love trees. . . .
      I could make him a tree picture.
      I could get him a tree seedling.

I could . . . none of this has anything
              to do with Serendipity.

I'm feeling hopeless   until I slip my hands
        into my jacket pockets.

        I remember Garrett's quick hands
        when my fingers close
        around a familiar object.

        A thimble.

Warm again.

I remember Mom's inscription
        about Dad—
        "who makes the world a poem"—
        and I think Yes.
        I am holding a kiss in my hand.

I keep the thimble tucked in my palm
        to give me strength
        when I face Dad inside.

Dad's bedroom door is open.

His leather bag is gone.

A short note on the kitchen table.
        Mrs. Whittier is home
        if you need her.

What I need is Dad here and a miracle.

Serendipity comes running
        stretches her paws out toward me
        her back end high in the air.

Then she drops loudly on her side
and rolls over to show me her tummy.

So cute.   Dad needs to see this.

I rub her tummy, then go to my room
to find a nest for the thimble.
I'm trying to think of some special way
to show Garrett how I feel
when I see—

there on my pillow
a stack of papers
in Mom's handwriting.

More of Mom's poems.

As I page through them
it strikes me
they're all about cats.

I pick up the first one to read.

SONNET FOR A CAT AND HER KITTENS

The musty-sweet smell of hay is in your
fur, kitty. A hint of where you've hidden
your babes. I know strangers are forbidden
to linger near the sun-dappled nest or
stroke the tiny tender noses before
you allow it, but I've watched your children
tussle in the night. Am I forgiven
if I explain that your son has a roar
like a dragonfly, and your daughters grow
more like you every day? Their faces draw
me; I can't help but climb up to the loft
while you're away and watch them swaying low
in their walk, or curling up on the straw
to sleep. They are my joy; so clean and soft.

I pick up another one. . . .

CATNAP

The cats are curled
like cinnamon buns
on the floor

like you could take
a giant spatula
and lift them
onto the plate
of your chair

like their sweetness
would sticky
the flat of your hand

like the steam
of their warmth
would rise
in clouds
of aromatic
dreams

I keep reading
        until I'm cat-saturated.

It's hard to believe
        she wrote
                this many poems
        about cats.

It's hard to believe
        I didn't know
        this side of her.

Does this Dad-offering
        mean I'm forgiven
        for making him sad?

I guess he's reaching out
        the best he can
        right now

sharing a bit of Mom
    with me.

I wonder if he'll tell me
        in his own words
        why we can't have a cat.

Unless maybe these poems
        are supposed to be
        his silent answer.

Because she loved them.

Inspiration hits.
　　　　I am a poet's daughter.
　　　　Maybe I can convince my dad
　　　　　　through a poem
　　　　　　that we need this cat.

I try to think of how I can write
　　　　all the reasons in a poem.
　　　　But my mind and the page
　　　　　　stay blank.

Serendipity mews near the window
　　　　and an idea bursts in my head.
Maybe a field trip
　　　　will start my brain working.

I grab a notebook and pen
　　　　tuck Serendipity under my arm
　　　　for her first trip

to the backyard.

Right away
     when I set her down
     she rolls in the dirt.

She's not exactly
     the princess type.

But at least I get
     a warm-up poem out of it.

A TRIP OUTSIDE

Maybe if you weren't
so white
I wouldn't know when you got
so dirty.

You look like a cloud
that is thinking
it ought to rain.

You look like a marshmallow
dunked in hot chocolate
and dropped in the dirt.

You look like a pile of socks
someone should put
in the wash.

I thought I only
        took my eyes off Serendipity
        for a second

        but when I look up from the page
        she's gone.

I scan the yard.
        I call her name.
        Does she know her name?

I walk the edges in a quick-step
        looking behind bushes
        up into trees.

How could she disappear
        so quickly?

I think she's too little
        to climb the fence
        but then I see something

that makes my heart bang:

a kitten-sized hole in the fence
the side that leads
to the front of the house
and the street.

She could be anywhere.

It's close to dinnertime.
Somehow the light changed
while I've been searching.

No sun.
The gray of dusk is closing in
and a feeling of impending fog.

I race out the gate
for a quick look in the front yard
but no one is there

no little white shape
to turn and greet
or even startle and dash

only silence and emptiness.

Dad! I start to yell

before I even get in the front door.

I find him in the kitchen.
>He turns with the phone in his hand
>and a strained expression on his face.

I can't find Serendipity.

He doesn't seem to take this in.
>*When were you going to tell me*
>*that Taylor wasn't taking the cat?*

What?

He hangs up/bangs up the phone.
>*Taylor's mom just called to say*
>*you left your sweater at their house.*
>*I asked her if she'd made her mind up*
>*about Serendipity*
>*and she thought I was kidding.*

He throws out his hands.
>*She's allergic, Sara.*
>*There was never any chance*
>>*they were going to take the cat.*

I'm not sure which disaster is worse—
 Serendipity's disappearance
 or the uncovering of the plot.

Dad, she's gone.

Dad looks at me
 then shuts his eyes.
 I can't abide lying
 he says.
 Maybe now
 things will get back
 to normal.

I can't believe what I'm hearing.
Normal? You want things back to normal?
I can feel my voice rising
    like a crazy person's.
What was so great about normal, Dad?
    I don't remember that
    making you happy.

Dad's face drops, but his eyes stay stern.
    She is not your cat.
    You knew that from the start.
    How could you sneak around
        behind my back?

That is too much.
    You're a great one for talking
        about sneaking around.
    I know about you and Mom.

Dad closes his eyes like he has a headache.

You're a child.
You don't know anything.

That's because you won't tell *me anything!*

He shakes his head hard and turns
     the usual cowardly direction
     toward his room.

It's becoming clear—
     he's not going to help me find her.
     He doesn't care if she's lost forever.
     He doesn't care how scared I am.

I reach for the doorknob.
I will go outside
     and find her myself.

He hasn't done
     his standard disappearing act yet.
     Sara, he says, *go to your room.*

My mouth drops open.
     No, I have to find her.

Go to your room.   *Now.*

I think my heart has just become
     a dumping place
     for sharp and heavy rocks.

How can he be so mean?
     She's lost.

What's so wrong about wanting
     a cat in my life?

I shouldn't have to lie
     in order to get one.

Serendipity is lost
     and I'm being sent to my room?

I stand at my window and look out on the street
     hoping that I'll see her.
But even the trees are disappearing
     in the fog.
Soon I won't be able to see anything.

It's another stupid Tule fog.
Well, I'm not going to stand here
     and let it kill Serendipity, too.
I'm not going to stay here
     while she's out there
     alone.

My dad showed me
     how to remove the window screen
     in case there was a fire.
Knowledge is as powerful as fairy dust.

     I'm gonna fly.

I try not to think of the trouble
     I'm going to get into.

I'm not sure what's happened to me
     since Serendipity showed up.
I used to do everything my dad told me to
     just to keep him from losing it.

But things are different now.

I feel like Joan of Arc.
     I know I'm on the side of right.
     I won't give in
     even if I'm burned at the stake.

Fortunately, that's not going to happen.
I'll probably just be grounded
     for the first time in my life.

But it will be worth it

because I will know
I've put someone else's life
before my own.

Someone soft and sweet
who needs my help.

I will be a hero.

I struggle a bit with the screen.
      I hope Dad can't hear me.

When the final clip is turned
      I pull the screen toward me
      and lean it against my bed
      leave my soft pink room
      for the spooky night.

It's easy to climb out of the window
      no prickly plants to scratch me
      no leap to the ground
         since it's only one floor
      no shaky rainspouts to climb down.

If I were my dad
      I might think about planting a rosebush
      right here
      so it wouldn't be so easy

for my daughter

to escape.

As I slip out the window

I see the fog slipping in. . . .

I start with a wide sweep
    around the fog-shrouded yard.

    No Serendipity.

I look toward the street
and hope-pray she's still close by.
I need to look deeper.

I'm searching under the bushes
    at the side of the lawn
    chanting, *Please, God*
    please, God   please, God
    when I hear Dad's voice
    coming through my window.

Sara? And then he must have noticed
    the open, screenless window frame
    because his voice sounds panicked
    as he calls my name out into the dark.

And I realize he can't see me
through the blanket of fog—
has no idea how far I've gone.

Maybe he thinks I've run away from home.

My gut tells me, Answer him
but my brain says, No.
If I go in now, I won't have Serendipity
and I'll still be in trouble.

I keep searching.

Fog water collects on the leaves and washes my hands
as I rifle the bushes hoping for a glimpse
of bright white.

My sweatshirt sleeves and my tennis shoes
are getting wet
making me feel cold and squishy.

I focus on finding Serendipity.

Still   I can't help but hear him.

I can't help but hear him
        crashing out the front door
        his footsteps racing away from me
        toward Mrs. Whittier's lit-up house.

He knocks normally at first.
        I can imagine him
        trying to keep it together
        trying to be calm and rational.

        But Mrs. Whittier doesn't answer
        and soon he is banging on her door
        and calling out to her.

Still no answer.
She must have left lights on
        when she went
        to pick up her stepdaughter.

Dad stops banging and shouting

but I can hear him breathing hard

and I hear him gasp, *Sara*

and I hear him pounding to the curb
and calling my name out through the fog
louder and louder
in his terrible panicky voice.

Sara, he cries over and over
and something in my chest cracks

but I stay stubbornly by the bushes
and think of Serendipity
and how much she needs me.

Then I hear Dad moan
    Not you   too

and that is more than I can bear.

I run to his voice.
    Daddy, I'm here.
    I'm sorry.

He wraps me in his arms
     and breathes *Thank you*
     into the top of my head
     only he's not talking to me.

     And he sobs like I haven't heard
     since those hopeless nights
     the first few months after Mom died

     and that makes me cry.

     We're an awful wet mess together
     sodden by the heavy fog
     and our tears.

Don't ever do that again, he gets out
     and I shake my head.
Never, don't ever do that again.

I won't.

He pulls my face up in both hands.
> *Why is that cat*
>> *so important to you?*

It's not just the fog
> that feels like it's suffocating me.

I tell him the hard truth.
> *I get so lonely, Dad.*
> *I need someone to hold on to.*

Dad's whole body seems to droop
> and I realize I'm finally telling him—

he hasn't been there for me.

He sighs and reaches his arm
> around my shoulders.

Then he walks me through the fog
> back into the house.
> *There's something*
> *I have to tell you.*

Dad sits me down on the couch.
>   *Your mother died*
>   *driving in fog like this.*

I know, Dad.

He puts up his hand like a stop sign.
But you don't know about before. . . .
We had a special cat—that orange one.
When MacLeish died—
He closes his eyes.
Mom cried for three days.
>   *I didn't ever want to*
>   *go through that again.*
So for years when she brought up
>   *getting another cat*
>   *I just refused.*
Dad looks at me.
Your mom finally convinced me.
And she wanted to surprise you.

She was on her way to get a kitten
    when the accident happened.

That explains a lot.
Now I miss her even more.

But wait.
    Dad, she wanted us to have a cat.

Dad nods.
    This is what I'm telling you.
He's quiet for a minute.
    I'm also telling you
        why I couldn't have a cat here. . . .
    I thought it would remind me too much
        of what I lost.
    I thought having a cat without having her
        would be too hard.

I don't want to ask but I need to know.
    Is it?

Dad's voice cracks.
    It's hard, Sara.

This is a tragic story
    and the rocks in my heart get sharper
    but I can't help but hear
        he didn't say   *Too hard.*

Does it make me a bad person
    to hear hope
    while we're talking about
    my mother dying?

Dad, I start
    but I don't know what to say.

He gets up for a box of tissues.
When we're drier   he says,
    She's scared and hiding right now.
    I doubt we'd ever find her tonight.
    But tomorrow. . . .

This is not a good time
　　　to argue.
I wasn't finding her outside
　　　anyway.

I stare at Dad
　　　afraid to ask.

He stares back.
　　　You were wrong
　　　to lie to me, Sara.
　　　And you were wrong
　　　to look through my things.
　　　And you were wrong
　　　to leave your room.

　　　But I was wrong, too,
　　　not talking about Mom
　　　not letting you have a cat.

I wait

hoping, hoping.

Your punishment is
    you are grounded for two weeks.
My punishment is
    you can have a cat.

I jump into his arms.
    I love your punishment,
    I tell him.
    Thank you, Daddy.

I can finally have a cat
    but the one I want
    is gone.

Dad tells me not to worry
    but how can I not?

She's a baby
    out there alone.

I finally drift off to sleep.
    Am I dreaming?

She is calling at the back door
    and sharpening her claws
    on the doorjamb.
She wants in so badly
    she flings herself
    like sticky tape

at the screen door
claws hook and hold

and she is stuck
clinging
hanging
singing a sad song

impossible to ignore.

I wake up suddenly.
Was I dreaming
        or did I really hear something?

I go out to the kitchen
        and there in the morning light
        hanging on the screen door
        is Serendipity.

Serendipity!
        I run to detach her.
        Her body swings out
        when I open the door
        but she is truly stuck.

Dad comes to the rescue
        lifting each claw
        from the tiny steel squares.
See? What did I tell you?

She knows a good thing
when she sees it.

I cradle Serendipity in one arm
and use the other
to give Dad a hug.

I know a good thing
when I see it,
too.

How to hold a sleepy kitty . . .

. . . in the nap of your arm

near the crook of your dream

in the armchair of your tenderness

on the pillow of your heart. . . .

It's maybe six months later. . . .

Dad hands me one of the tennis racquets
        that live near the front door—
        within easy reach for our game time.

We leave the lights on in the family room
        to welcome us when we return
        and wave at Mrs. Whittier
        through her picture glass window.

We walk past Mom's dorm
        in the campus dark.

Dad's carrying his racquet like a banjo
        and the bright lights from the courts
        make him look like a shiny country star.

He stops to see if Serendipity will pause.

She's following us

slipping beneath the dew-moistened bushes
raising the smell of wet leaves and earth.

She thinks she's invisible
he says, grinning.
But she's not.

Her whiteness glows against the dark.
She's a fluffy ghost
on a moonlit mission.

We begin to play
pretending we don't see her.
Each twang on the racquet
makes her tail jump
as she crouches at the end of the net
waiting.

And then the ball falls into the net
and she races to it
jumps on it
throws it in the air
and flies for freedom to the other side.

We can't help laughing

at our little kitty
Serendipity

like we do so often
these days.

Acknowledgments

Many, many thanks to the following people (and cats):

my kind and patient agent, Stephen Fraser, who loved this story when it was still a picture book and he was still an editor;

my wonderful cat-loving editor, Joy Peskin, who guided me to find the story beneath the story;

my other thoughtful editor, Catherine Frank, who helped me finish the process;

my critiquers and writing buddies, especially Janet Settimo, Peggy Reiff Miller, Mary Ann Moore, Doris Holik Kelly, Peggy Archer, Tracy Burchett, Diane Sutton, Erin Harden, Kathy Higgs-Coulthard, Kirsten Klassen, Carol Brodtrick, and George Ella Lyon;

my savior, who came to give us abundant life;

my parents, Sam and Barbara Marsh, who indulged the pet cravings of their daughters;

my husband, Marc, and my sons, Brendan and Corey, who are just as tickled by cat antics as I am;

my extended family, who have shared many a cat laugh with me, especially my sister-aunt, Kathy Hatchett-Toohey;

and finally, the cats I have lived with—Thomasina, my first cat; Stinky, the original dorm kitty; Jasmine, the fluffy white cat; Princess, the ever-reigning queen; Winnie, my first grandkitty; and Max and Murray, the cornfield boys.

I love you all.